Rosie Sips Spiders

Alison Lester

For Lachlan

Houghton Mifflin Company
Boston 1989

Work

Ernie is a wildlife photographer.

Celeste is a famous ballet dancer.

Frank is an astronaut.

Cowgirl Rosie
"from the Kimberleys
to Kosciusko"
℅ P.O. Coopers Creek

Ernest Zebratrak
Photographer
of
Wild Animals

Her Royal Highness
Princess T

Astral
Exploration
with
Frank.

Rosie goes herding.

Nicky is the doctor at the doll's hospital.

Clive bakes chocolate cakes.

But Tessa is a princess.

 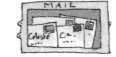 

Rosie lives in a
trailer.

Tessa owns a
castle.

Clive has a house
on stilts.

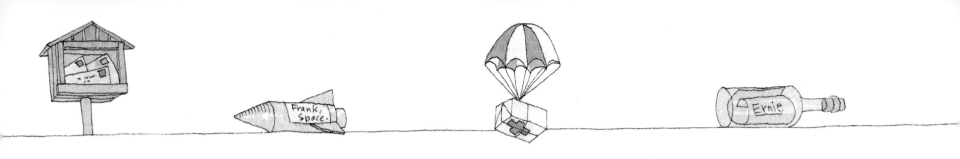

Ernie's home is a boat.

Celeste lives in a skyscraper.

Nicky lives on an island.

But Frank lives on the moon.

Favorite food

Clive eats fried rice.

Nicky loves spaghetti.

Celeste enjoys lemon meringue pie.

Ernie likes roast
beef.

Tessa has baked
Alaska.

Frank eats space
rations.

But Rosie sips spiders.

Having fun

Ernie likes beach-combing.

Tessa hosts the royal ball.

Rosie sings with her band.

Celeste feeds the
ducks.

Frank studies
astronomy.

Clive practices
karate.

But Nicky loves to fly.

Gardens

Frank has a rock-
garden.

Rosie tends a
cactus.

Ernie collects
carnivorous plants.

Clive waters a
window box.

Tessa has a maze of
roses.

Nicky grows
hibiscus.

But Celeste has a secret garden.

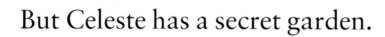

Animals

Nicky swims with a
dancing dolphin.

Clive has a baby
crocodile.

Rosie works her
cattle dog.

Celeste talks to her
cockatoo.

Tessa has a tame
tiger.

Frank has an ant-
farm.

But Ernie has a menagerie.

Baths

Celeste soaks in her
sunken tub.

Ernie showers
under a tree.

Frank has a bubble
bath.

Nicky shares her
tin tub.

Tessa wallows in a
marble bath.

Rosie has a scrub in
the horse-trough.

But Clive jumps into Alligator Creek.

Sleep

Tessa stretches out on a four-poster bed.

Clive curls up in a sleeping bag.

Frank sleeps in his space ship.

Nicky's bed is out
on the porch.

Celeste has a heart-
shaped bed.

Ernie snores in a
hammock.

But Rosie sleeps beneath the stars.

Printed in Hong Kong
10 9 8 7 6 5 4 3 2 1

The author wishes to thank Rita Scharf of Oxford
University Press for her assistance with this book.

Library of Congress Cataloging-in-Publication Data

Lester, Alison.
    Rosie sips spiders / Alison Lester. — 1st American ed.
        p.   cm.
    Originally published in Australia in 1988 by Oxford University
Press — T.p. verso.
    Summary: Each child in this group of seven likes to do everything
in an individual way whether it's work, taking a bath, playing, or
going to sleep.
    ISBN 0-395-51526-2
    [1. Individuality — Fiction.] I. Title.·
PZ7.L56284Ro   1989   89-1821
[E] — dc19   CIP
                                   AC